DUBS

GOES TO

PHILADELPHIA

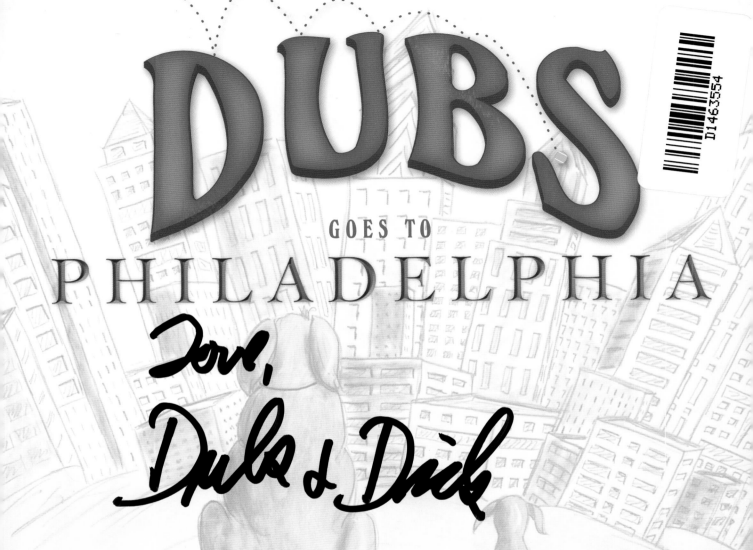

Dick Morris · Eileen McGann · Clayton Liotta

Illustrations by Clayton Liotta

Requests for permission to make copies of any part of the work should be submitted online at info@velocity-press.com or mailed to Velocity Press, Suite 1000, 49 Twin Lakes Road, South Salem, NY 10590.

Library of Congress Cataloging-in-Publication Data is pending.

Printed in the United States of America.

ISBN: 978-1-938804-05-2

www.velocity-press.com

Velocity Press

Here are some other books I've written as part of my
DUBS DISCOVERS AMERICA series:

Dubs Goes to Washington

and

Dubs Runs for President

The sun was shining, it was a beautiful day,
And Dubs and Daisy were happily on their way.
It had been so fun to dream of a Presidential race,
But right now they were excited to visit America's birthplace.
So it was on to Philadelphia, the City of Brotherly Love,
A town where history and democracy go hand-in-glove.

It all started at Independence Hall,
Where Dubs and Daisy played some ball.
Here the Declaration of Independence was signed,
Creating a country of a whole different kind.
Where once there were royals who ruled over our lands,
Now the people took power in their very own hands.

To call lawmakers together, the Liberty Bell would ring,
Alerting citizens to meetings and other important things.
The bell was a symbol of our free, independent nation,
And a part of the spirit of every celebration.

After independence, they wrote a Constitution
To set up a fabulous new governing institution.
We went to the National Constitution Center so that we could see
How this new Constitution has made us all free.
We have free speech, free press, and dogs have the right
To bark anytime—but never to bite.

Ben Franklin Court was his home in the city,
And it was here on this spot that he discovered electricity.
He also invented the world's first stove,
So up to his door the furry pair drove.
His house stood straight; it was three stories tall,
And had a great yard in which to play ball.

Dubs tried to imagine what Philadelphia was like
Before there were cars or even a bike.
In Elfreth's Alley were houses from the eighteen hundreds,
Is this how things looked? Dubs had always wondered.
If you had come here in 1802
You'd have met blacksmiths and glassblowers, to name just a few.

While they wrote the Constitution and the grand Declaration,
Betsy Ross sewed our first flag with a special decoration:
A field of deep blue with thirteen white stars,
And to honor the colonies, thirteen red and white bars.
Dubs wore this great flag designed by Ms. Ross
Around his furry gold neck to show he was boss.

The Continental Congress first met in Carpenters' Hall,
And here, Dubs and Daisy played a quick game of ball.
When it came to a ballgame, they were quite a good match.
Neither could throw, but they knew how to catch.

At the Philosophical Society, men spoke of new things.
They were finished with tyrants and bullies and kings.
Folks should be free, they certainly all knew,
And Dubs thought dogs should be part of that, too.

Thomas Jefferson wrote our famous Declaration
That created our brand new democratic nation.
Dubs and Daisy visited Graff House, the place where he stayed.
As he wrote the Declaration, he was never afraid.
Neither Dubs nor Daisy had written anything at all,
But they were better than Jefferson at playing with a ball.

From 1790 to 1800, Congress met at Congress Hall.
Now Daisy, this is no time to play with that ball!
During its time the Hall hosted many important events,
Including the inauguration of two presidents.

Philadelphia is packed with history galore!
All these great sights—who could ask for anything more?
With the memories of Jefferson, Franklin and the rest,
This trip has certainly been one of our best.

But where should we go next? I have a good thought:
To a place where big battles had often been fought.
A place where our settlers were put to the test.
I think we should pack up and head out West!

Dear Reader:

I hope you had fun reading about Philadelphia, which is called the City of Brotherly Love. They should have said Sisterly Love, too, but Daisy says we know they meant that, so we'll give them a break.

When you have time, draw something on the inside of the front cover that reminds you of Philadelphia. Or anything else you'd like to draw. Or paste some pictures there. We love drawings and photos!

If you have not seen our other books, you might want to take a look. Our first trip was to the nation's capital, called DUBS GOES TO WASHINGTON, where I tried to find my lost tennis ball. Boy, that was not easy, as you will see.

Then I decided to run for office in a book called DUBS RUNS FOR PRESIDENT. What a crazy time that was, running against Felix the Cat! Guess who won? You'll be surprised how that came out.

Tell me what you think about my adventures, or anything else you want me to know. All you have to do is email me at Dubs@DubsTheDog.com or visit me at Facebook.com/DubsTheDog. I'm a Golden Retriever! I love my pals!

Okay, Daisy and I have to go now, our soup bone is waiting.

Your friend,
Dubs